Heidi

FAMILY LEARNING

from Dorling Kindersley

The Family Learning mission is to support the concept of the home as a centre of learning and to help families develop independent learning skills to last a lifetime.

Project Editor Natascha Biebow
Senior Art Editor Jane Thomas
Senior Editor Marie Greenwood
Managing Art Editor Jacquie Gulliver
Picture Research Victoria Peel and Jamie Robinson
DTP Designer Kim Browne
Production Joanne Rooke

Published by Family Learning

Dorling Kindersley registered offices:
9 Henrietta Street, Covent Garden, London WC2E 8PS

VISIT US ON THE WORLD WIDE WEB AT:
http://www.dk.com

ISBN 0-7513-7067-3

Colour reproduction by Bright Arts, Hong Kong
Printed in Italy by L.E.G.O.

A CIP catalogue record for this book is available from the British Library.

Acknowledgements
The publisher would like to thank the following for their kind permission to reproduce their photographs:

a = above; c = centre; b = below/bottom; l = left; r = right; t = top.
Ace Photo Agency: Mauritius 29; Edmund Nagele 44 br; Ronald Toms 44-45; **AKG London:** 35, 46, 47 br; **Artothek:** Walter Klein 25; **Bridgeman Art Library, London/New York:** Elgin Court Designs Ltd, London: The Goatherd, c.1920 by Julius Paul Junghann (1876-1953) 10; **Britstock-IFA:** Bernd Ducke 31; **Jean-Loup Charmet:** 14; **Mary Evans Picture Library:** 45 tr, cl, 47 bl; Institution of Civil Engineers 46-47; **The Ronald Grant Archive:** *Heidi,* 1952 48 br; **Robert Harding Picture Library:** 45 tl; **Hulton Getty:** 45 bc, 47 cl; **Image Bank:** Hans Wolf 4; **The Moviestore Collection:** *Heidi,* 1937 © 20th Century Fox Film Corporation 48 bc; **Peter Newark's Military Pictures:** 48 clb; **Norfolk Rural Life Museum:** 45 br; **Rätisches Museum Chur:** 44 bl, 45 cr; ©**Retrograph Archive Ltd:** 19; **Roger-Viollet:** 47 tr; **Schweizerisches Landesmuseum Zürich:** 9, 12, 45 c; **Science & Society Picture Library:** 39; **Johanna Spyri Museum:** 48 tl; **Jürg Winkler (Museums-Stiftung Hirzel):** 48 cra.
Jacket: **Image Bank:** Hans Wolf back; **Johanna Spyri Museum:** inside back.

The publisher would particularly like to thank the following people:
Andy Crawford and Gary Ombler (photography); Sallie Alane Reason (additional illustration); Claire Ricketts (design assistance); Nick Turpin and David Pickering (editorial assistance); Marilyn Schaffner, Johanna Spyri Museum.

YOUNG CLASSICS

Heidi

By JOHANNA SPYRI
Retold by **Sally Grindley**

Illustrated by **Pamela Venus**

Family Learning

Contents

Up the Mountain

ONE SUNNY June morning, Heidi trudged
wearily up the mountain behind her Aunt
Detie. It was very hot, but the little girl was wearing all her
clothes at once as though it were winter. As they walked through
a village, a voice called out, "Detie, isn't that the orphan your sister
left? Where are you taking her?"

"I'm taking her to live with her grandfather," replied Detie.
"I can't look after her any more because I'm starting a
job in the city."

"Poor Heidi," said the villager. "No-one else
will go near that miserable old hermit!"

While Detie gossiped with the villager,
Heidi skipped away to play with Peter the
goatherd. As he did every morning in the
summer, Peter had come to the village to fetch
the goats and take them to graze in the rich
green meadows above. At first, he ignored Heidi.
She scrambled behind him up the slopes, puffing
and panting under the weight of all her clothes.
Then she unwound her thick scarf, and took
off her boots and both her dresses. She laid
them in a neat pile and danced after
Peter wearing only her petticoat.
He couldn't help smiling

Heidi skipped away
to play with Peter.

then. "How many goats have you got?" asked Heidi, and,

"Where are you taking them?" She chattered away until they reached Peter's hut and Detie caught sight of her.

"What on earth have you been doing, Heidi?" she scolded. "And where are your clothes?"

"I don't need them," protested Heidi. "I want to run around free like the goats."

Detie tutted crossly and sent Peter back to fetch the clothes; then they carried on climbing. It took another hour to reach Grandfather's hut. Three huge fir trees stood behind it, and in front, on a wooden seat overlooking the valley, sat the old man.

Heidi ran straight to him and held out her hand.

"Hello, Grandfather," she said. He took her hand gruffly and stared at her intently.

"Good morning, Uncle," said Detie. "I've brought Heidi to stay with you. It's your turn to look after her now," she said, and explained why.

The old man stood up angrily and said, "My turn is it? Well then, you go back where you came from, and don't come here again in a hurry."

Detie quickly said goodbye to Heidi and ran off down the mountain.

"Hello, Grandfather," said Heidi.

The old man sat in silence, while Heidi explored her new home. She ran round the back and found an empty goat stall, then stood enjoying the sound of the wind whistling through the trees.

"Can I see inside now?" she asked, when she came back round to the front of the hut.

Her grandfather showed her into a biggish room with a table and one chair, a bed, and a stove. A cupboard in the wall held everything he owned. Heidi pushed her clothes right to the back.

"Where shall I sleep, Grandfather?" she asked.

"Where you like," he replied.

In a corner by his bed was a ladder. Heidi climbed up and discovered a hayloft filled with fresh hay. "I'll sleep up here," she said. "Come and see how lovely it is, Grandfather."

She shaped the hay into a mattress and pillow, while her grandfather brought her the covers from his own bed.

"Time to eat now I think," he said.

Heidi watched him toast a large piece of cheese over the fire in the stove. Then he sat Heidi on a three-legged stool and turned his chair into a table for her. On it, he placed a mug of milk and a plate with a slice of bread covered with the toasted cheese. Heidi couldn't believe how good everything tasted.

That afternoon, she followed the old man everywhere, and watched as he

Mountain huts, like Grandfather's, had strong wooden frames and small windows to keep out the cold and wind.

carved a chair specially for her. When dusk fell, Heidi heard a shrill whistle and Peter appeared with his goats. With a shout of glee, she rushed to greet her friends of the morning. Two goats went straight to her grandfather, who held out salt for them to lick. Heidi patted them gently as Peter led the others away.

"Are these ours, Grandfather?" she asked. "What are their names?"

"The white one is Daisy and the brown one is called Dusky," replied her grandfather. "Now, young lady, it's time for bed."

"Good night, Grandfather. Good night, Dusky and Daisy," cried Heidi as she ran indoors.

Heidi was fast asleep.

That night, the wind howled so hard that the hut creaked and branches fell from the fir trees. The old man climbed up to make sure Heidi was all right. In the light of the moon he watched her sleeping, the expression on her face one of pure happiness.

Peter's shrill whistle woke Heidi the next morning. Eagerly, she jumped out of bed and ran outside, where Peter was waiting to collect Daisy and Dusky.

"Do you want to help Peter with the goats?" asked Grandfather.

"Oh, yes!" cried Heidi.

Grandfather gave Peter some bread and cheese for Heidi's lunch. "Mind you keep a close eye on her," he warned as they set off.

It was very beautiful on the mountain that morning. Heidi darted about picking flowers, and the goats, sensing her joy, ran here, there, and everywhere. Peter needed eyes all round his head to keep watch on them and Heidi.

In summer, goatherds led their herds up the mountain to feed on the rich grasses there.

At last they reached the foot of a rocky peak. Peter fell asleep in the sun while the goats grazed. Heidi gazed at the mountains above, which seemed to have faces like old friends. Suddenly, she heard a loud shriek overhead. "Peter! Peter! Wake up!" she cried. "Look at that bird! Why is it so noisy? Where is it going?"

"That's the hawk going home to its nest," answered Peter.

"Let's climb up and see where it lives," said Heidi.

"Not even the goats go that high," laughed Peter. "Come on, it's time for lunch."

Peter's lunch was tiny compared with Heidi's. To his amazement, Heidi gave him her share and seemed quite content with only two big mugs of Daisy's milk.

"What are the names of the goats?" she asked, while Peter enjoyed his feast.

Peter told Heidi about all the goats. She was sad when she heard that one of the little goats called Snowflake had lost her mother. Heidi promised to take special care of her.

By now the sun had begun to set, spreading a golden glow across the mountain tops. Heidi looked up in astonishment.

"Peter," she cried. "The mountains are on fire!"

"It's always like that," said Peter. "Tomorrow you can see it again. It's time to go home now."

During supper that evening, Heidi was full of questions. Grandfather said the hawk shrieked to tell people in the villages to stop making trouble for one another. He told her the names of the mountains and that the fire was the sun saying good night. That night, Heidi dreamed of mountains and flowers and of Snowflake.

Heidi darted about
picking flowers.

All summer long Heidi went to the pasture with Peter. She grew strong and healthy and carefree as a bird. But when the autumn winds came, she had to stay at home. "We don't want you being blown off the mountain," said her grandfather.

So she spent the days watching him make cheese and build things with wood.

They flew down the snowy mountain.

Then the snows came. Heidi gazed out as the snowflakes fell faster and faster and buried the hut up to the window-sills. "I hope the hut will be buried completely so that we have to light a lamp during the day," she laughed.

Peter was at school during the week now, but one Sunday he came by to say his Grannie would like Heidi to visit her. Heidi begged to go the very next morning, but the snow was too deep. When the snow finally froze and the sun came out, Grandfather wrapped Heidi up warmly, sat her on his sledge, and they flew down the mountain, screeching to a halt outside Peter's tiny hut.

While Grandfather made his way back up the mountain, Heidi went inside. An old woman was bent over a spinning wheel.

"Hello, Grannie," said Heidi. "Here I am at last. Grandfather brought me on his sledge."

Grannie felt for Heidi's hand while Heidi looked about the room. "One of your shutters is hanging

Village women spun their own yarn from goat's or sheep's wool using a sturdy, wooden spinning wheel.

loose, Grannie," she said. "Grandfather will mend it for you."

"I can't see it, my dear, but I can hear it banging," said Grannie.

"Why can't you see it, Grannie?" asked Heidi.

"I can't see anything, child, light or dark, sun or snow. I shall never see them again."

Heidi began to sob. "Can't anyone make you see?" she cried.

"I can't see, but I can hear," said Grannie, softly. "Come and tell me what you and Grandfather do up on the mountain."

Heidi brightened up. "Just wait till I tell Grandfather about you. He'll be able to make you see, and he'll mend the hut, too. He can do anything." She chattered away about everything she did and how clever Grandfather was and all the things he had made, until Peter came in and walked her back up the mountain.

As soon as she was indoors, Heidi told her grandfather about the shutter and begged him to mend it and to make Grannie see again. "Well, we can at least stop the banging," he said.

All winter long, while Heidi kept Grannie company, Grandfather hammered and sawed. Little by little, he repaired the whole hut, but Heidi had to learn that he couldn't make Grannie better. ❋

"Here I am at last, Grannie," said Heidi.

Detie Comes Back

T HE WINTER PASSED and another happy
summer. Towards the end of Heidi's second
winter, an old man dressed in black arrived at
the hut.

"Good morning, pastor," said Grandfather,
pulling up a chair for him.

"I'll come straight to the point," said the pastor.
"Heidi should have gone to school this winter. The
teacher sent you a warning but you didn't reply."

"She's not going to school," replied Grandfather. "She'll grow up
here with the goats and the birds, who
won't teach her any bad ideas."

"Heidi should go to
school," said the pastor.

In winter, village children
went to school to learn to
count, read, and write. In
summer, they had to help
their families earn a living.

"They won't teach her to read and
write, either," said the pastor.

The pastor did everything he could to
make Grandfather change his mind, but
Grandfather insisted Heidi should stay
with him up in the mountains.

The following day, however, they had
another visitor. It was Detie, dressed from
head to toe in fine new clothes. She
started to talk at once. "How healthy Heidi looks. You've certainly
looked after her well. Of course, I always intended to come back for
her. Anyway, now I've found a wonderful opportunity for her with a
rich family in Frankfurt. She's to be a companion to a little girl
who's confined to a wheelchair . . . "

"Have you quite finished?" interrupted Grandfather, rudely.
"Heidi's happy where she is."

Detie was furious. "Only someone who doesn't care about her

could keep her from such good fortune.
You won't even send her to school or
church. Well she's my sister's child and I'm still
responsible for her."

"Then take her," thundered Grandfather.
"But don't ever bring her back."

"You've made Grandfather very angry,"
said Heidi, as he stormed out of the hut.

"He'll get over it," said Detie. "Collect
your clothes, you're coming with me."

"I'm not coming," said Heidi, "I want to
stay here with Grandfather." But Detie was
determined. She hauled Heidi off as fast as
she could with promises that she could
come back in a day or two with fresh rolls
for Grannie. Heidi couldn't even say
goodbye to Peter.

Detie didn't stop to
talk to anyone in the
village, and before she
knew it, Heidi found
herself aboard the
train to Frankfurt.

*Detie hauled Heidi off
down the mountain.*

When they arrived in Frankfurt, Detie took Heidi to a house belonging to a wealthy man called Mr Sesemann. His daughter, Clara, was an invalid. Her mother had been dead for a long time, and Mr Sesemann was often away on business, so Clara was left in the care of the housekeeper, Miss Rottenmeier.

When they arrived, Detie and Heidi were shown into the study, where Miss Rottenmeier came to inspect Clara's new companion. She was not impressed by Heidi's shabby dress and straw hat, and even less impressed by her name.

"Surely that's not your proper name," she said.

"She was christened Adelheid, after her mother," explained Detie.

"Then she will be called Adelheid," said Miss Rottenmeier. "And how old is she? I told you we wanted someone of Miss Clara's own age, which is twelve."

In the middle of it all, Heidi fell asleep.

Detie pretended not to be sure, but Heidi piped up, "I'll soon be eight. Grandfather told me so."

When Miss Rottenmeier learned that Heidi couldn't read, she shook her head in disbelief and said, "She really won't do at all." But Detie stressed that Heidi was just the sort of unusual child Miss Rottenmeier had said she was looking for, and quickly took her leave.

While Miss Rottenmeier was out of the room, Clara asked Heidi, "Do you want to be called Heidi or Adelheid?"

"Everyone calls me Heidi – that's my name," said Heidi.

"Then I'll call you Heidi," said Clara. "Are you glad you've come?"

"No," Heidi replied, truthfully, "but I

shall be going home tomorrow, with some nice fresh rolls for Grannie."

Clara laughed. "But you've come here to keep me company and to have lessons with me. They'll be much more fun now."

Miss Rottenmeier returned and snapped at the servants to serve the evening meal. Heidi was delighted to find a white bread roll by her plate. She asked one of the servants, Sebastian, if she could have it, and put it straight into her pocket. Then Sebastian held a dish of food out in front of her and she didn't know what to do, it was all so different from Grandfather's. Miss Rottenmeier launched into a long lecture on how she was to behave at the table, how she was to speak to the servants, and issued instructions about getting up, going to bed, shutting doors, keeping tidy, and so on and so on.

In the middle of it all, Heidi fell asleep. ❋

Heidi knows nothing about table manners. She's never even used a knife and fork. The white bread roll is a big treat.

Strange Goings-On

WHEN HEIDI WOKE the next morning in a big room in a high bed, she couldn't think where she was. Then she remembered – she had come to Frankfurt. She went to the bedroom window, but it was so high that she could only just peep out. All she saw were the walls of the buildings opposite. Heidi began to feel frightened.

At breakfast, Heidi asked Clara, "How can I look out of the window and see what is down below?"

Clara explained that the servants would open a window for her if she wanted, then asked Heidi to tell her about her life at home.

Heidi chattered longingly about the mountains and goats and all the other things she loved, until Clara's tutor, Mr Usher, arrived and began teaching Heidi the alphabet. It wasn't long before a tremendous clatter brought Miss Rottenmeier running.

"Heidi thought the carriages were fir trees rustling and knocked over the ink in her rush to see them," said Clara, smiling behind her hand.

"Does she think Frankfurt is in the middle of a wood?" exclaimed Miss Rottenmeier.

She stormed off to find Heidi and scolded her roundly.

That afternoon, Heidi was relieved to learn she could do as she liked while Clara rested. She asked Sebastian to open a window. "There's nothing but stony streets," she said sadly. "Where can I go to see the whole valley?" she asked.

"Somewhere high, like that church tower over there," Sebastian told her.

Heidi ran out of the house to find the church

Heidi asked a hurdy-gurdy player to show her the way.

Poor city boys often earned a living by playing a hand organ called a hurdy-gurdy. It made music when the handle was turned.

tower but soon got lost. She asked a hurdy-gurdy player to show her the way. "Clara will pay you if you come to the house," she promised.

When they got to the church tower, Heidi begged the keeper to let her climb up. But all she could see from the top were chimneys and roofs. Seeing how disappointed she was, the keeper showed her a basket full of kittens. "You can have them," he said. "I'll deliver them to your house."

"Oh, yes, please," said Heidi. "Can I take two of them now?"

The keeper nodded. Heidi put the kittens in her pocket and skipped back home. When she got inside, she found everyone in the dining-room waiting to eat. "Why did you leave the house without permission?" asked Miss Rottenmeier severely.

"Miaou," seemed to be Heidi's reply. "Miaou, miaou."

Miss Rottenmeier almost choked with anger. "How dare you make fun of me!" she screeched.

"It's not me, it's the kittens," Heidi protested, and held them up.

Miss Rottenmeier screamed and ran from the room. She was terrified of cats. But Clara adored the kittens. She begged Sebastian to hide them, so she and Heidi could play with them later.

"Leave it to me, Miss Clara," said Sebastian, chuckling.

All Heidi saw from the tower were chimneys and roofs.

The next morning, Sebastian went to the front door to find a ragged boy with a hurdy-gurdy on his back, holding a tortoise.

Miss Rottenmeier hates cats, but other families kept them to chase away mice and rats that ate their food stores.

"I've come for the money Clara owes me," he said.

"How can Miss Clara owe you money?" asked Sebastian, rudely.

"I showed her the way to the tower yesterday," said the boy. Sebastian began to grin.

"What's Heidi been up to this time?" he wondered. "All right," he said out loud. "I'll let you in if you'll play a tune for Miss Clara." He led the boy to the study, where Clara and Heidi had begun their lessons. The boy set down his tortoise, and began to play.

In a room close by, Miss Rottenmeier pricked up her ears. "Where's that dreadful noise coming from? It sounds as if ..." She ran to the study and stood by the door, horror-struck. "Stop that at once!" she cried. She ran across the room and tripped over the tortoise, then screamed for Sebastian who, doubled up with laughter, put some coins into the boy's hand and led him away.

Before Miss Rottenmeier could find out who was responsible for this latest outrage, Sebastian reappeared with a big basket for Clara.

"For me?" said Clara in surprise.

"Finish your lessons first," said Miss Rottenmeier.

Clara didn't have to wait long to find out what was inside the basket. It wasn't fastened properly, and suddenly there were kittens everywhere. They bit Mr Usher's trousers, climbed up Miss Rottenmeier's skirt, and scrambled onto Clara's chair.

"Oh, aren't they pretty little things!" exclaimed Clara.

"Sebastian!" screamed Miss Rottenmeier.

"Get rid of these dreadful creatures."

It wasn't until the evening,

when Miss Rottenmeier had recovered a little, that she got to the bottom of the morning's disturbances. She turned to Heidi, who was quite unaware that she had done anything wrong. "I can think of only one punishment for a dreadful child like you," she said. "Perhaps a spell in the dark cellar among the bats and rats will change your ways."

But Clara protested loudly. "Oh, please, Miss Rottenmeier. Wait till Papa comes home. I'll tell him everything and he'll decide what's to be done with Heidi."

Reluctantly, Miss Rottenmeier agreed.

"Get rid of these dreadful creatures," screamed Miss Rottenmeier.

For a few days there were no further mishaps. But Heidi was beginning to feel terribly homesick. Then she remembered that Detie had told her she could go home when she wanted. One afternoon, she wrapped up the rolls she had been saving, put on her old straw hat, and went to the front door. Just at that moment, Miss Rottenmeier saw her.

"Where do you think you're going, dressed like that?" she demanded.

"I want to go home to see Grandfather and Grannie," murmured Heidi.

"What? You'd simply run off? What's wrong with this house, pray? You're an ungrateful girl who doesn't know when she's well off."

*Miss Rottenmeier
scolded Heidi for
trying to run away.*

At this, Heidi burst out, "I want to go home because the goats and Grannie will be missing me and here I can't see the sun saying good night to the mountains, and if the hawk flew over Frankfurt he'd shriek louder because so many people are horrid and cross."

"The child's out of her mind!" exclaimed Miss Rottenmeier.

She called for Sebastian to take her to her room. He tried to cheer Heidi up by promising to take her to play with the kittens, but that evening Heidi didn't eat a thing, though she put a roll in her pocket as usual.

Worse was to come the following day. Miss Rottenmeier decided to give some of Clara's outgrown dresses to Heidi before Mr Sesemann came home. She went to look through Heidi's own clothes to see what was worth keeping. There, in the cupboard, she found the hoard of rolls. She immediately ordered one of the servants to throw them away, together with Heidi's old straw hat.

Coarse, brown bread is hard for Grannie to chew, so Heidi has been saving expensive soft, white bread rolls for her. She does not realize they will go hard and stale.

"No!" Heidi wailed when she heard what was happening. She threw herself down by Clara's chair and sobbed, "Now Grannie won't get any nice white bread."

Clara did her best to console Heidi. "I promise to get you just as many rolls as you have saved to take to Grannie when you go home. And they'll be soft fresh ones, not hard and stale ones like those you've been saving. Please don't cry any more, Heidi."

It was a long time before Heidi could stop crying, but at last she understood what Clara was saying and felt comforted. That night, when she went to bed, she found her old straw hat under the quilt. Sebastian had rescued it for her. ❊

Mr Sesemann Comes Home

THERE WAS great excitement in the house a few days later when Mr Sesemann returned from his travels laden with presents. He greeted Clara affectionately, then held out his hand to Heidi.

"So this is our little Swiss girl," he said. "Tell me, are you and Clara good friends? I hope you don't squabble."

Mr Sesemann arrived laden with presents.

"Clara is always good to me," said Heidi.

"And Heidi never quarrels with me," said Clara.

"Good," said Mr Sesemann. "Now as soon as I've had something to eat, I'll come back and show you what I've bought for you."

He went along to the dining-room, where Miss Rottenmeier greeted him with a face like thunder. "Things are not well here, Mr Sesemann. Heidi is quite unsuitable for Miss Clara. Her conduct is beyond belief, and you should see the sort of people and animals she has brought into the house. I can only think she's not quite right in the head."

"She seems normal enough to me," said Mr Sesemann, and then, as Mr Usher came into the room, he continued, "Perhaps you can help, Mr Usher. Tell me plainly what you think of Heidi."

"So this is our little Swiss girl," said Mr Sesemann.

Like this businessman being met by his children, Mr Sesemann is delighted to see Clara again. He is often away on business, but gives Clara lots of attention when he is home.

Mr Usher started rambling on about Heidi being behind in her education and a little unusual in her conduct, but he took so long to come to the point that Mr Sesemann excused himself and went to find Clara.

"What's been going on while I've been away?" he asked her.

Clara told him exactly what had happened, about the hurdy-gurdy player and the kittens, the rolls and everything else. When she had finished, her father laughed out loud.

"So you don't want me to send Heidi home?"

"Oh no, Papa," cried Clara. "Since Heidi's been here, delightful things have happened nearly every day."

Mr Sesemann went to find Miss Rottenmeier. "Heidi will stay," he said firmly. "The child seems perfectly normal and Clara loves having her here. If you find her too much to manage, my mother will be arriving soon and she can manage anyone."

Mr Sesemann was only home for a fortnight, but soon after he had left, a letter arrived to say that old Mrs Sesemann would arrive the following day.

"Since Heidi came, delightful things have happened," Clara told her papa.

Late the next day, Grandmamma Sesemann arrived. Heidi saw such a kind expression on the old lady's face that she loved her at once.

While Clara was resting the following afternoon, Grandmamma asked Miss Rottenmeier to fetch Heidi so that she could give her some books.

"Books!" exclaimed Miss Rottenmeier. "In all the time she has been here, she hasn't even learnt her alphabet, as Mr Usher will tell you."

"That's strange," said Grandmamma. "Well, she can at least look at the pictures."

Heidi soon appeared. She loved looking at the beautiful books. Then, all of a sudden, she burst into tears when they came to a picture of a green meadow with animals grazing, a shepherd, and a setting sun.

When she saw the picture of the green meadow, Heidi burst into tears.

"Come, my dear, don't cry," Grandmamma said gently. "Dry your eyes and we'll have a chat. Tell me, what have you learnt in your lessons?"

"Nothing," sighed Heidi. "Peter told me it was too difficult, and it is."

"But you musn't simply take his word for it. You must try hard yourself. As soon as you can read, I will give you this book."

Books were very expensive, so only rich people like the Sesemanns could own them. Heidi is upset because the picture reminds her of home.

Heidi's eyes shone when she heard this. "I wish I could read now!" she exclaimed, and for a few moments she was happy.

But Heidi had begun to realize that she couldn't just go home when she wanted to. She believed Mr Sesemann would think her ungrateful if she asked to go away, so she didn't tell anyone how she felt. When she was alone in her room, she often lay awake thinking of the mountains, and then she would dream about being home and wake up crying because she was still in Frankfurt.

When Grandmamma noticed her tears one morning, she asked her why she was so sad.

"I can't tell you," said Heidi. "I can't tell anyone."

"If we can't tell an ordinary person our troubles," said Grandmamma, "then we can tell God and ask Him to help us."

That night, Heidi knelt by her bed and begged God to help her go home.

❋

One morning, about a week later, Mr Usher came to Grandmamma with the news that Heidi could read at last. She went to the study to find Heidi reading to Clara. "I can do it!" exclaimed Heidi excitedly. "Now I can read stories about all kinds of people and things."

That evening, at supper, Heidi found the big picture book beside her place. "It's yours now," said Grandmamma, "even when you go home." ❋

Heidi was in the study, reading excitedly to Clara.

Home Again

WHEN GRANDMAMMA LEFT, strange things began to happen in the house. Every morning the front door was found wide open, even though it had been locked and bolted. Nothing was ever stolen and there was nothing to show who had opened it. Miss Rottenmeier asked Sebastian and John, the coachman, to spend a night downstairs to see if they could discover the cause of the mystery.

Evening came, and the two men sat up and waited, but there were no unusual sounds. At one o'clock, John went out into the hall to check. Almost at once, a gust of wind blew out his candle. "The front door is wide open," he stammered, "and there was a white figure on the stairs which vanished."

A cold shiver ran down Sebastian's spine.

As soon as Miss Rottenmeier heard their story, she wrote to Mr Sesemann asking him to come home.

Two days later, Mr Sesemann arrived home. He summoned his friend Doctor Classen to help him keep watch that evening. They chuckled at the idea of a ghost, but settled down to wait anyway. At about one o'clock in the morning,

they heard the sound of a bolt being pushed back. They rushed out into the hall. The front door was open and a streak of moonlight shone on a white figure standing there.

"Who's there?" shouted Dr Classen.

The figure gave a little cry. It was Heidi, in her white nightgown.

"What are you doing here, child?" asked Mr Sesemann in astonishment.

"I don't know," answered Heidi faintly.

"I think this is a case for me," said Dr Classen. He took Heidi gently by the hand and led her upstairs to bed.

"Have you been dreaming?" he asked her.

"Oh, yes," said Heidi. "I dream every night that I'm back with Grandfather, and I get up to see the stars shining, but when I wake up I'm always still here in Frankfurt." Tears began to stream down her cheeks.

"Have a good cry," said Dr Classen. "Then go to sleep and in the morning everything will be all right."

He went to find Mr Sesemann. "Your ghost is Heidi sleepwalking," he said. "She's terribly homesick and has lost a lot of weight. You must send her back home – that's the only cure."

Mr Sesemann immediately began preparations for Heidi's journey home. Clara was very upset when she heard, but her father promised she could visit Heidi soon.

It was Heidi in her white nightgown.

Doctors often sent their patients to the mountains to rest – but Dr Classen sends Heidi back to the mountains because she's ill from missing her home there.

Heidi couldn't believe she was going home at last. Sebastian accompanied her on the long train journey, then arranged for her to travel to the village with the baker on his cart. Her arrival caused a stir among the villagers, who were amazed that she was going back to Grandfather of her own accord.

Heidi ran first to Peter's tiny hut, where Grannie was sitting in her usual corner. "It's Heidi, Grannie," she cried, and threw herself on Grannie's lap and hugged her. "I'll never go away again and I've brought you fresh rolls from Clara and I'll visit you every day," said Heidi.

"How wonderful!" exclaimed Grannie. "But you're the best present ever."

"I must go to Grandfather now," said Heidi excitedly. "I'll come again tomorrow."

Heidi continued her climb. Soon she could see her grandfather's hut. He was sitting on the bench outside, just like the first time she saw him. Heidi ran to him crying, "Grandfather!" and threw her arms round him. For the first time in years, his eyes were wet with tears.

"I've brought you fresh rolls," cried Heidi.

"So you've come back, Heidi," he said. "Did they send you away?"

"Oh no, Grandfather," said Heidi. She tried to explain what had happened, then from her basket she fetched a letter and a packet from Mr Sesemann. Grandfather read the letter and said, "The packet's for you, Heidi. There's money in it for you to buy a bed and anything else you may need."

"I don't need it," said Heidi, and then she cried excitedly, "but I can use it to buy fresh rolls for Grannie to have every day!"

Just then she heard a shrill whistle, and saw Peter with the goats. He stared at her in astonishment and said, "I'm glad you're back."

The church was at the centre of village life. After church, people exchanged news and chatted. Grandfather now wants to be a part of this life once more.

Heidi greeted the goats, then ran inside the hut, where she found that Grandfather had made up her old bed in the loft. That night, she slept soundly for the first time since she'd been away.

Grandfather woke her in the morning wearing his smartest clothes. "Put on your best dress," he said, "and we'll go to church together."

They set off down the mountain hand in hand, and when they entered the church, people turned to stare at them. At the end of the service, Grandfather spoke to the pastor. "I have changed my mind. I shall move down to the village for the winter so that Heidi can go to school."

The pastor smiled, and the villagers saw them part like old friends. They crowded round them. "We're so pleased to see you among us again," they said.

When they started back home, Grandfather said to Heidi, "I never thought I would be this happy again. It was a good day when God sent you to me."

After the service, Grandfather spoke to the pastor.

As dawn broke one September morning, Heidi was woken by a fresh breeze rustling the tops of the fir trees. She leapt out of bed and went to watch her grandfather milking Dusky and Daisy. Peter soon came up the path with the rest of the goats and asked, "Are you coming with me today?"

"I can't, Peter," said Heidi. "My nice people from Frankfurt might arrive."

She had been saying the same thing for days, and Peter was fed up with it. He went grumpily on his way, while Heidi spent the morning tidying the hut. When she came out, she looked down the mountain slope and cried, "Grandfather! They're coming!" She had recognized the doctor and rushed to greet him. "Doctor! Thank you a thousand times for sending me home to Grandfather." Then she looked down the path and asked, "Where are Clara and Grandmamma?"

"I'm afraid I've come alone," said Dr Classen. "Clara has been very ill and isn't fit to travel. They'll come in the spring when it's warmer."

Heidi was thrilled with all the wonderful gifts.

Heidi and Grandfather eat simple, wholesome food, such as brown bread and cheese. The sausage the doctor brought is a luxury.

Heidi was very upset at first, but brightened up at the thought of showing the doctor all the things she loved. "Come and meet Grandfather," she said.

The two men shook hands warmly and sat down with Heidi on the seat outside the hut. "I hope you'll spend as many of these beautiful autumn days as you can up here," said Grandfather. "I'll be your guide over any part of the mountains you wish to see."

He disappeared indoors and soon brought out a steaming jug of milk and golden cheese. The doctor ate his meal with great relish and said, "This is certainly the place for Clara to come to get well."

Just then a man arrived with an enormous parcel. "Ah," said the doctor. "Now you can have fun unpacking your gifts from Clara."

Heidi was thrilled when she found cakes and a shawl for Grannie, a huge sausage for Peter, tobacco for Grandfather, and all sorts of surprises for herself.

The weather was glorious all that month. The doctor came up to the hut every day from the village where he was staying. Sometimes he went off on long walks with Grandfather who told him all about the plants and wildlife. Other days Heidi took him up to the pasture, where she chattered away about the goats and the mountains, or recited verses she had learnt by heart.

All too soon it was time for the doctor to return to Frankfurt. Heidi walked a little way down the mountain with him, until he stopped and said, "I wish I could take you back with me to Frankfurt."

Heidi thought for a moment and replied, "It would be nicer if you came back to us." ✳

Winter in the Village

GRANDFATHER KEPT his promise to move to the village in the winter so that Heidi could go to school. As soon as the first snow fell, he took Heidi and the goats down to the village, where they rented a ramshackle old house that he had spent the autumn repairing. Heidi eagerly explored all over, until she came to a room with panelled walls and a huge white stove in the corner. Behind the stove was an alcove, and there was her bed, made up just as it had been at the hut. "Oh, Grandfather," she exclaimed happily, "my room! Isn't it lovely?"

Heidi missed the mountains, but she soon felt at home. Each morning, she leapt out of bed to visit Dusky and Daisy in their stall at the back. Then she went off to school and worked hard at her lessons.

Peter was hardly ever at school. One lunchtime, when he burst in to tell Grandfather that the snow was now hard enough for Heidi to visit Grannie, Heidi asked, "Why weren't you at school again today?"

"I couldn't stop the sledge and went straight through the village," said Peter dramatically, "and then it was too late."

"Do that again and

Heidi went to school and worked hard at her lessons.

you'll get what you deserve from me," said Grandfather sharply. "Now have something to eat, then Heidi can go and visit Grannie."

When Heidi climbed back up the mountain with Peter, she was upset to find Grannie ill in bed. She did her best to cheer her up by reading hymns, and that night she lay in her own bed thinking that if only she could read to her every day she might help to make her better. Then she had an idea that pleased her so much she could hardly wait till morning to carry it out.

Peter went to school the next day. On his way back, he dropped in at Grandfather's as usual. As soon as he was inside, Heidi caught hold of his arm and said excitedly, "I've thought of something. You must learn to read properly."

"Can't be done," said Peter.

"I'm going to teach you," said Heidi, "and then you can read to Grannie every day, especially when the snow is too deep for me to visit her."

Peter refused at first, but when Heidi pointed out the problems he would have if he didn't learn, he at last agreed. With the rhyming ABC book that Clara had given her, Heidi taught Peter the alphabet, then a few words, until one day, he astonished Grannie by reading

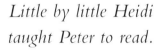

Little by little Heidi taught Peter to read.

her a whole hymn. Soon the whole village heard how Grandfather was responsible for getting Peter to school, and how Heidi had taught him to read. ❋

Peter is convinced he will never read, but Heidi helps him learn his letters with an alphabet book like this. Once he knows his ABC, he can sound out words, then sentences.

The Unexpected Happens

A S SOON AS spring came and the mountainsides were green again, Heidi and Grandfather moved back to the hut. Heidi gleefully explored her old haunts until Peter arrived with a letter from Clara. Heidi read it out. "They'll be here in just over six weeks' time," she said excitedly.

The prospect of more visitors from Frankfurt made Peter angry. Grannie too seemed troubled when she heard the news. She feared that Heidi's friends would take her away again. But Heidi knew nothing of this, and could hardly wait for the end of June. At last, one morning she went out of the hut and suddenly shouted, "They've come! They've come!"

Grandfather saw two men carrying a chair on poles and on it a little girl carefully wrapped up. Behind them rode a stately woman on horseback, while two more men pushed a wheelchair and carried an enormous bundle of rugs. Heidi sped over the grass to hug Clara. Grandmamma dismounted and greeted Heidi, then turned to Grandfather. "What a magnificent place to live!" she exclaimed.

Grandfather spread some rugs on the wheelchair, lifted Clara in his strong arms, and gently settled her into it. Straightaway, Heidi pushed the wheelchair round the hut to show Clara the fir trees and the goat stall and the flowers that grew all around.

"Oh, Heidi!" cried Clara. "If only I could run about with you."

"Don't worry," said Heidi, "I'll push you everywhere."

Grandfather fetched out the table and chairs and they sat eating toasted cheese and drinking great mugs of milk in the gentle breeze.

After the meal, Heidi took Grandmamma inside the hut. Grandfather carried Clara up the ladder to Heidi's bedroom. "Oh, Heidi," she cried, "I never imagined such a lovely place to sleep! Fancy being able to lie in bed and look at the stars."

Grandfather glanced at Grandmamma. "Why not leave Clara with us for a time while you stay in the nearby village of Ragaz?" he suggested. "I promise to look after her, and you can come and visit whenever you please."

Clara and Heidi were overjoyed at the idea, and Grandmamma beamed at Grandfather. "I was thinking myself how much good it would do Clara to stay here. What a kind fellow you are!"

With that Grandmamma set off, and Heidi and Clara helped Grandfather prepare supper.

"They've come! They've come!" cried Heidi.

The days with Clara passed quickly. Grandfather grew very fond of her, and he tried to find something new every day to make her better. He instructed Peter to let Daisy feed on the very best grass so she would give extra good milk to make Clara strong. Then, when Clara had been there for a fortnight, Grandfather began trying to get her on her feet. At first she gave up quickly because it hurt, but each day she tried for a little longer.

Heidi told Clara about the pasture where Peter took the goats and begged Grandfather to take them there.

"I will if Clara tries to stand on her own this evening," he smiled.

Heidi rushed to tell Peter. "We're coming up to the pasture with you tomorrow."

But Peter only growled and hit the ground with his stick. Heidi had not been to the pasture once that summer, and now she was only coming to show it to her new friend. He wished Clara would go away so that everything would be the way it was before.

When he went up to the hut the next morning, Peter saw Clara's empty wheelchair waiting outside. No-one was around. In a sudden burst of rage, he sent it plunging down the steep slope. Then he dashed up the mountain without Dusky and Daisy.

Grandfather and Heidi came out of the hut a few moments later and searched everywhere for the chair. Then Grandfather looked down the mountain and saw it in pieces a long way below.

Peter pushed the wheelchair down the mountainside.

Clara slowly put one foot in front of the other.

"It must have been the wind," said Heidi.

"Now I won't ever be able to go up to the pasture," wailed Clara.

"We'll go up anyway," said Grandfather, and then he remarked, thoughtfully, "Peter is very late."

Grandfather picked up Clara and an armful of rugs and they began the trek up to the pasture with Dusky and Daisy. Peter was already there. Grandfather scolded him for leaving the goats behind and asked, "Did you see Clara's chair?" Peter shook his head.

Grandfather left Clara and Heidi in a sunny place on the grass, where they spent the morning as happy as can be. After lunch, Heidi thought of the meadow higher up. "Oh, you must come with me to see the flowers, Clara," she said. "I'm sure Peter and I could carry you."

Peter felt so guilty that he agreed to help. They hauled Clara to her feet, and slowly but surely she began to put one foot in front of the other. "Look at me!" she cried. "I'm walking!"

When Grandfather came to collect them late that afternoon, his face lit up at the news. But Peter went home with a heavy heart. He was terrified when he saw villagers standing round the broken wheelchair.

Peter is so jealous of Clara's friendship with Heidi that he pushes her chair down the slope. Without her chair, Clara tries even harder to walk.

The next day, Clara and Heidi wrote to Grandmamma and begged her to come and see them in a week's time. They didn't say why. Clara spent all week practising her walking, until the big day finally arrived.

The girls sat down outside the hut to wait for Grandmamma in a state of great excitement. At last, she came into view. When the old lady saw the children, she cried out, "Why Clara, where's your chair?" and as she came towards them, she said, "How well you look!" Then Heidi stood up – and so did Clara, and they walked before her. Grandmamma stared in amazement. Half laughing, half crying, she hugged Clara, then Heidi, then Clara again. Seeing Grandfather, she turned to him and said, "How can we ever thank you! It's your care that has done this."

"How well you look!"
cried Grandmamma.

"And God's good sun and His mountain air," added Grandfather.

Grandmamma decided to send a telegram telling Clara's father to come immediately. "I shan't tell him why," she said.

Grandfather whistled for Peter to deliver it. Almost at once, Peter came running down from the mountain, white as a sheet. He feared that the awful moment had come when he would be arrested. He was greatly relieved to find he only had to deliver a message.

As he was running down the path to the village, a man beckoned to him. Peter stopped in his tracks but wouldn't go near. "Come along, lad," shouted the poor traveller. "Can you tell me if this path

Clara blossoms under Grandfather's good care. The fresh mountain air and healthy food have given her the strength to walk again.

leads to the hut where the old man lives with a child called Heidi, and where some people from Frankfurt are staying?"

"A *policeman*!" thought Peter. He was so terrified that he dashed off down the mountain, tripped, went head over heels, and landed in a bush.

"How shy these mountain folk are!" Mr Sesemann said to himself, and continued on his way. He had finished his business trip early and was planning to surprise Clara by landing unexpectedly on Grandfather's doorstep.

Peter, in the meantime, had lost Grandmamma's telegram and was scrambling back up the mountain as fast as his bruises and his guilty conscience would let him go. He wanted to run and hide under his bed, but Grandfather had told him to hurry back to look after the goats, and he didn't dare disobey the old man's orders.

Peter was so terrified that he dashed off down the mountain and tripped.

Mr Sesemann chuckled when he saw Grandfather's hut a little way above him. "What a surprise they'll have when they see me!"

But he had already been spotted. An excited group stood outside the hut waiting to surprise him instead. As he drew nearer, two girls came towards him, a tall fair one leaning slightly on a smaller dark one. He stood still and stared, and suddenly his eyes filled with tears.

"Don't you know me?" Clara cried.

At that, he strode towards her and took her in his arms. "Is it possible?" he cried.

Grandmamma joined them. "Come and meet Heidi's grandfather."

Mr Sesemann thanked Grandfather with all his heart for restoring Clara's health.

While they were talking, Grandmamma saw Peter trying to slip past. "Young man," she called. "Why are you so frightened to come near us?"

Peter stared at the ground, looking ashamed.

"I think you'll find Peter was the 'wind' that blew Clara's chair away," said Grandfather suddenly. He had

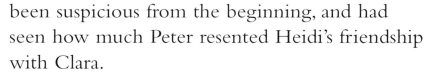

Mr Sesemann took Clara in his arms.

been suspicious from the beginning, and had seen how much Peter resented Heidi's friendship with Clara.

Grandmamma listened to what had happened, and took Peter aside. "What you did was very bad," she said, "but I understand what you must have been feeling. Now, I want you to choose something to remember us by."

Peter couldn't believe he could choose anything he liked. He thought and thought, then asked for a penny. Grandmamma laughed, and promised him a penny a week

Grandmamma caught Peter trying to slip past.

for the rest of his life. Peter thanked her and skipped off joyfully.

Later, Mr Sesemann said quietly to Grandfather, "Is there any way in which I can show you my gratitude?"

"I, too, am overjoyed at Clara's recovery," said Grandfather. "But if you could promise me that when I die you will take care of Heidi, that would richly reward me." Mr Sesemann gave his word and the two men shook hands on it.

All too soon, the time had come for Mr Sesemann, Clara, and Grandmamma to leave. Clara began to cry, but Heidi said brightly, "It'll soon be summer again and then you'll come back, and you'll be walking right from the beginning. Just think what good times we'll have!"

Heidi stood at the edge of the slope and waved goodbye till they were out of sight.

Nor was that all. Shortly afterwards, the doctor retired and came to live in the village. He bought the ramshackle house that Grandfather and Heidi had lived in, and had it rebuilt so that he could live in one half and they could use the other half in the winter.

"I have come to love Heidi almost like my own child," the doctor told Grandfather one day. "May I help you take care of her?"

Grandfather took the doctor's hand in his, and said, "That would be wonderful!"

So Heidi spent another happy winter in the village, surrounded by all those who cared for her.❄

The doctor offered to help
take care of Heidi.

Heidi's Mountain Home

HEIDI'S STORY BEGINS when she goes to live with her grandfather in the mountains in Switzerland. Life with Grandfather is simple and carefree. Heidi spends her days outdoors in the fresh air, tending the goats with Peter and helping Grandfather with his chores.

❋ MOUNTAIN VILLAGE

Grandfather lives high up in a mountain range called the Alps, and rarely goes down to the village below. The villagers gossip about him because they don't understand his ways.

❋ VILLAGE CHILDREN

In summer, village girls helped with household tasks, while boys worked on the land or, like Peter, tended sheep and goats. In the winter, children were free to attend school. Because she lives so far away, Heidi can only go to school when Grandfather moves down to the village.

It snows a lot in the Alps in winter. The only way to reach remote huts like Grandfather's was with a sled or on skis.

✼ MOUNTAIN HOME
Grandfather's hut has only one room, so Heidi has to sleep in the hayloft. It is simply furnished, and like this one, has a log fire for cooking and heating.

Milk pail

Ladle

Bowl

Grandfather toasts cheese for Heidi using a long, wooden fork.

✼ CARPENTER
In mountain areas, wood was used to build homes and make household objects. Many village men made their own furniture and utensils out of wood, like Grandfather does.

✼ WHOLESOME FOOD
Mountain people ate simple but healthy food, such as soup, brown bread, and cheese. Like many villagers, Grandfather makes his own cheese from goats' milk. He sells the cheese in the village so he can buy brown bread and meat.

The cheesemaker went from farm to farm helping to make cheese.

Goats are fearless climbers, well-adapted to the mountains.

Clara's City Home

HEIDI GOES TO STAY with Clara in the busy German city of Frankfurt. Clara's family is rich, and they live in a big house that has many rules. Heidi finds it hard to remember all of these, and she often does things that horrify Miss Rottenmeier. Heidi is often indoors, and misses the freedom and fresh air of her mountain home.

Most of the time, children were expected to remain silent unless spoken to.

The nursemaid helped the housekeeper to look after the children.

Grandmothers often lived with or visited their families.

The master of the house sat at the head of the table.

❀ FAMILY MEALTIME

Wealthy families had servants to serve meals and do the housework. In Clara's house there is a housekeeper, a butler, a maid, and a coachman. A cook makes rich foods with much meat and fish. Heidi is overwhelmed by all this, and doesn't know how she should behave.

It took two days to travel between Heidi's village and Frankfurt.

❋ FRANKFURT

Heidi has never been to a city before, and cannot understand why there are buildings all around. She feels trapped inside Clara's house because she can't see the sky or the mountains. Clara tries to make Heidi feel at home.

❋ CITY HOME

Clara's family lives in a big Frankfurt house with many rooms, including a dining-room, a sitting room, and a study. This is a big change for Heidi, who is used to Grandfather's one-room hut.

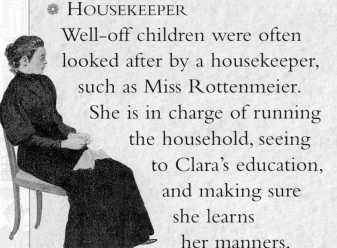

❋ HOUSEKEEPER

Well-off children were often looked after by a housekeeper, such as Miss Rottenmeier. She is in charge of running the household, seeing to Clara's education, and making sure she learns her manners.

❋ TUTOR

Only rich families could afford a tutor like Mr Usher. He teaches Clara reading, writing, and maths. After a difficult start, he teaches Heidi how to read, too.

Johanna Spyri

JOHANNA SPYRI WAS BORN IN 1827, in the small Swiss village of Hirzel. Just like Heidi, she and her five brothers and sisters lived a healthy, outdoor life in the mountains. She tended the family's goats, and sometimes helped her father, who was a country doctor.

The old schoolhouse in Hirzel

Johanna Spyri (1827–1901)

Heidi was written to help men wounded in war.

❋ WRITING FOR CHILDREN

After she married in 1852, Johanna Spyri began writing children's books to earn money to help the men wounded in the Franco-Prussian War. In 1880, her first novel, *Heidi*, was published. It was a big success. Spyri wrote almost 50 other books, but none was as well-loved as *Heidi*.

❋ A POPULAR STORY

Heidi was translated into English in 1884 and soon became popular all over the world. It inspired several film versions: in 1937, Shirley Temple starred as Heidi, and in 1952, Elspeth Sigmund played the same role.

Shirley Temple

Elspeth Sigmund